To the independent shopkeepers,
who serve our communities

The Corner Shop

Liz Hedgecock

WHITE
RHINO
BOOKS

ISBN-13: 979-8337573847

1

Saffron was about to hit the snooze button again when she registered that the bedroom was light. Far too light for the time of day it ought to be. 'Damn,' she whispered, rolled out of bed and headed straight for the en suite. No time to wash her hair: dry shampoo would have to do.

I shouldn't have waited up, she thought, as she removed a layer of skin with a body mitt. *Flaming Americans. Flaming Americans who can't make decisions.* She turned off the water, grabbed a towel, wrapped herself in it and glanced in the mirror.

God, you look tired. She opened the bathroom cabinet and gazed wistfully at the Crème de la Mer and Touche Éclat. *Only for special occasions*, she said firmly to herself, as she reached for the supermarket dupe moisturiser that was really quite good. And worlds cheaper.

Having assumed a protective layer, and added both lift and volume to her hair (which should have been highlighted two months ago to stay on schedule), she put on her white waffle bathrobe and went to the bedroom door. 'Aurora! Chad! Breakfast time!' Then she went downstairs, made herself a strong black coffee, took her vitamins and put out breakfast bowls and glasses of milk.

Chad was down first, a small scruffy thunderbolt yawning fit to bust. He picked up the cornflake packet and filled his bowl to the top.

'Are you going to eat all that?'

'Yeah.' He reached for the milk, then paused. 'Are these different cornflakes? They're the wrong colour.'

'No,' said Saffron. 'Same box, see. Maybe they changed the recipe. They do that sometimes.'

'Oh.' He flooded the bowl with milk.

'Any sign of your sister?'

He turned and yelled 'Roar!'

Saffron winced. 'There's no need to shout and your sister's name is Aurora.'

He grinned. 'Everyone calls her Roar. Even the headteacher.'

Saffron just resisted putting her head in her hands. *So much for picking names that couldn't be shortened.* Instead, she went to the foot of the stairs. 'Aurora! You'll be late for school if you're not careful.'

On the little table in the hall were three letters which had arrived yesterday. They were unopened. She had left them because the kids were with her, and she needed a positive mindset for the call with New York, and, well, because. Two bills, one with red writing on the envelope, which she had moved to the bottom. The other was a letter from her ex-husband's solicitors. 'More good news, no doubt,' she muttered, and ripped it open.

Dear Ms Montgomery,

We are writing to remind you that from the first of July, your maintenance payments will reduce. This is due to a change in the financial circumstances of your former husband. As we wrote previously, this will represent a reduction of £825 in your monthly payments.

If the situation changes, we will of course keep you informed. Please contact us if there is anything you wish to discuss.

Perhaps it was the coffee, but Saffron's muscles tensed and her heart banged in her chest. She forced herself to take deep slow breaths and stuffed the letter in her bathrobe pocket. 'Aurora!' she yelled. 'Get up *now!*'

'I am up,' Aurora protested. 'I'm doing my sun salutation.'

'Never mind that, you should be eating your breakfast.'

Eventually, both children were breakfasted and in their school uniforms – Aurora's skirt was well above her knees, suggesting yet another growth spurt – and Saffron was suitably armoured in skinny jeans, high-heeled ankle boots and a Breton top. 'We'll have to drive,' she said. 'Shoes on.'

Chad shoved his feet in his shoes without untying the laces. 'Oh Chad, you'll ruin them.'

'No I won't,' said Chad. 'Everyone does it.'

'That doesn't mean you have to. Come *on*, Aurora.'

Aurora was making a face at her left foot, encased in its regulation T-bar shoe. 'It doesn't fit.'

A chill gripped Saffron. 'Don't buckle it so tight.'

'I'm *not*. I can hardly get my foot in. I definitely can't wiggle my toes like the shoe lady says.'

Saffron nearly expressed a very forthright opinion of the shoe lady. Instead, she examined the thickness of Aurora's ankle socks, which was no help at all. 'We've got three options. Make do as you are, try them without socks, or wear your trainers.'

'Trainers!' cried Aurora, and shot towards the shoe rack like a streak of lightning.

***

Saffron was fuming when she finally got the 4x4 off the drive. *Bad things always come in threes. How many is that?* Two bills, a solicitor's letter, new shoes,

4

and no doubt grumbles from school about the trainers. That made five, which meant something else was in store for her.

Positive thoughts. Deep breaths.

A driver drove out of the side road without looking and she leaned on her horn.

'This is what happens when you mess around before school,' she said, into the rear-view mirror. 'We have to be on the road with idiots and risk getting killed.'

'I can't help my feet growing,' Aurora said sadly. 'What are you doing today, Mummy?'

Working out how I can possibly afford new school shoes which will probably be too small by September, thought Saffron. 'I have calls with a couple of clients and I'll be working on a business expansion plan.' *If it's possible to expand a business which is practically dead on its feet in these interesting times.* 'Do you know what you'll be doing?'

'We're starting our new topic,' said Aurora. 'It's called Where We Live.'

'Oh, that sounds nice. What about you, Chad?'

'Dunno. Stuff.'

'Of course.' She turned into Beech Lane and passed the book swap, which was currently wearing a crocheted topper consisting of a large, striped worm wearing spectacles and reading a book. She rolled her eyes. *What some people find time to do.*

As they approached the school, both sides of the road were lined with cars.

'We've got to turn round,' said Chad. 'We can't park here.'

'No time,' said Saffron. She kept going, past the turning circle…

'Mummy!' cried Aurora.

'There's a space,' said Saffron, pulling on to the tarmac in front of the fence and parking behind a small red Peugeot.

'But Mr Sullivan says—'

'Mr Sullivan isn't trying to get you to school on time. Anyway, we'll just be a few minutes. The bell's about to go: hurry up.'

Both children took their own sweet time unbuckling the seatbelts and getting down from the car. Then Saffron noticed Aurora's laces were undone. 'Oh, for heaven's sake!' She knelt to tie them.

'Mum, I forgot my reading book,' said Chad. 'Can you—'

'No, I can't!' barked Saffron. 'Go to your lines before the bell rings.' She marched to the gate and held it open for them. 'Aurora, I'll talk to your teacher about your shoes.'

'Mrs Hanratty,' prompted Aurora.

'Yes, I know. Now go!'

'Scuse me.' It was a voice Saffron knew, and disliked intensely.

Standing halfway between the gate and the main entrance, arms folded in the manner of a bouncer, was Mr Sullivan, the school caretaker. 'Yes?'

'Those spaces are staff only at this time of day.' His face was neutral rather than angry, which somehow made her feel more as if she was being told off. By someone who was probably younger than she was.

'I'm sorry, I had no idea,' she said flatly.

'I'm pretty sure I've mentioned it to you, Mrs Montgomery.'

'Ms.'

'And it's been in the school newsletter more than once.'

She held up her hands. 'OK, I was in a rush.' *Unlike you, standing there in your scruffy jeans like the parking police.* He hadn't even shaved: his dark stubble was practically a beard.

'It's a matter of safety,' he said. 'I'd appreciate it if you could remember in future.'

By the time Saffron had thought of a suitably cutting reply, he was ambling to the school entrance. There was a big smear of green paint on his jeans. *What sort of example is that for the children?* Her eyes narrowed as she inspected his T-shirted top half. *Not to mention those sleeve tattoos.*

The bell rang, and she remembered the trainers. No doubt Mrs Hanratty would give her a lecture on

7

uniform standards. If she did, Saffron was ready to give her a piece of her mind. She tossed her bouncy hair and stalked towards the junior playground, head held high.

2

As it turned out, Mrs Hanratty was surprisingly sympathetic. 'Kids always grow out of things at the most inconvenient time,' she said. 'Of course Roar can wear her trainers if her school shoes don't fit any more.'

Saffron considered correcting her about Aurora's name, but decided to be merciful in the circumstances and merely said 'Thank you.'

Mrs Hanratty glanced around the playground at the dispersing parents and leaned closer. 'As it's the last half term, we have a policy that the children can wear trainers. No sense in buying shoes they'll only grow out of at this point in the year. We're spending most of our time on the field or the playground anyway, as the weather's so nice. So they'll practically all be in trainers.'

'That's good to know,' said Saffron. 'A very

sensible policy, given that some parents must be feeling the pinch.'

'Quite,' said Mrs Hanratty. 'Well, better go and teach the little darlings, I suppose.'

'Yes, and I must get to work,' said Saffron. 'My clients won't look after themselves.'

'Saffron!'

She turned. It was Heather, happily married fellow-menace of the PTA, a businesswoman who was going places. Since her divorce, Saffron had mostly avoided her. Too painful a contrast. 'Oh, hello. How are you?'

'Oh, fine, fine. Would you like a coffee? I've heard about something that may interest you. I don't have to be online until ten today.'

'Um, let me check my schedule.' Saffron took out her phone and consulted her blank calendar. 'Go on then. Luckily, most of today's clients are transatlantic.' *Nonexistent.*

'Excellent,' Heather said briskly. 'Let's go.'

***

They went to Café de Paris, in the village. Denise, the owner, was behind the counter. She gave Heather a pleasant smile, then beamed at Saffron. 'Welcome back! Have you been working away?'

'In a manner of—'

'Two cappuccinos and two almond croissants, please,' said Heather. 'My treat.'

'You really don't have to—'

10

'We'll be over there.' Heather led the way to a round table with two bentwood chairs, each with a cushion in a fifties-style print of chic women walking dogs.

Saffron wondered what the opportunity might be. Presumably she would be doing Heather a favour, since she was being taken out for coffee and croissants. She hoped it wasn't compliance training, her least favourite. Though of course she'd do it.

She leaned forward. 'How are you? We see each other in passing at the PTA meetings, of course, but everything's so busy.'

'Oh yes?' Heather's eyebrows lifted slightly.

'You know how it is. Clients on the go, always switched on...' Saffron tried not to wriggle under Heather's scrutiny.

'Times are hard,' said Heather. 'Right now, I'm putting the hours in just to keep things at the same level.'

A young server arrived with a tray. 'Two cappuccinos, two croissants,' he said, setting out cups, plates and cutlery rolled in a napkin.

'Thank you,' said Heather, and smiled at him. 'Let's tuck in, shall we.'

Saffron broke a small piece from the end of the croissant and put it in her mouth. Her brain flooded with images: savouring a croissant at the breakfast bar at home, as a reward for leading a coaching seminar

11

for a business in Germany. A treat bought in advance and consumed in bed after a talk on resilience delivered to a team in Sacramento. Late-night snack or very early breakfast, depending on your view. She had eaten in silence and darkness, not wanting to disturb David…

She looked at her plate. Half the croissant was gone. She picked up her cappuccino and sipped, then put it down. 'So, Heather, what can I do for you?'

'Do you know the little convenience store on the road to Meadborough? The Country Stores?'

Saffron frowned. She had seen the shop, on her way to Meadborough to get her nails done or catch a train to London, but had never visited it.

'It's on the corner. They have boxes outside with fruit and veg.'

'Yes, I know it.' Her eyebrows drew closer together and she made an effort to force them apart. If her frown lines deepened, there was no way she could get them fixed at the moment. What was Heather getting at? 'Is it part of a chain?'

'No, it's a husband and wife team. The kids used to help in the shop, but they live and work elsewhere now.'

'I don't see what—'

'Alf and Janet are getting on, and the shop's becoming too much for them. Janet fell off a kick stool when she was restocking the other day and sprained her ankle. I was in there buying emergency wellies – it's that kind of shop, sells everything – and they're desperate for a hand. But they don't want to go through the rigmarole of applications and interviews and all that.'

Saffron smiled. This was either a coaching assignment or a recruitment exercise. Fine. She could cope with that.

'I said I knew someone who might be able to help and told them I'd have a word.' Heather sipped her drink. 'So, would you be interested? It's within school hours, ten till two, Monday to Friday. They said they could pay eleven pounds an hour, maybe more for the right person.'

'Eleven pounds—' Saffron's jaw dropped. 'You mean you're asking me to – to work in the shop?'

'I know it isn't your usual line of work, Saffron,' said Heather. 'Alf said he'd be happy to show you the ropes. It's not like there would be systems to learn.'

'I – I—' For once, Saffron was speechless.

'Do you feel insulted?' Heather asked quietly. 'I'm sorry if you do. But you look as if you need help.'

'Not that sort of help,' snapped Saffron.

Heather reached for Saffron's hand and examined her nails. They were clipped instead of filed, painted with metallic bronze nail varnish which had gone clumpy and chipped at the tips. One nail was cut short. 'When was the last time you had a manicure?'

'I haven't had time!' Saffron wanted to cry. No, she wanted to run and hide where no one could catch sight of her or her raggedy nails and make assumptions.

'I know it's not what you're used to,' Heather said gently. 'Please think about it. I've recommended you, so they're bound to take you on. A steady job – an easy job – during school hours and out of the village. The chance of anyone from school seeing you is practically zero. And you could still do your own work around it, in the early mornings and the evenings.'

Saffron picked up her cappuccino and sat back. Eleven pounds an hour. Forty-four pounds a day. Over two hundred pounds a week, before tax. It would cover the shortfall in maintenance that was due to hit her next month.

'I didn't mean to, but I overheard your conversation with Mrs Hanratty,' said Heather. 'Times are hard for everyone, and if I can help…'

Saffron considered the alternative. Fewer companies were inviting pitches and tenders these days, and some of her most regular clients had either downsized or been absorbed into bigger companies with their own arrangements.

She saw herself buying the cheapest brands from the cheapest stores and refilling brand-name containers battered with use. Growing out her highlights. Telling the children that they couldn't go on the class trip because—

'I'll talk to them.' She seized the remains of her croissant and took a bite. But the croissant, which had always tasted of sweetness and sophistication and success before, was sickly and bitter. She took a swig of her cappuccino and managed to swallow it. Then she said 'Thank you,' which was even harder.

'It's a pleasure,' said Heather. 'We haven't seen as much of each other lately, but I couldn't help noticing, and I guess that the divorce—'

'Which was a good thing,' said Saffron. 'I'm better off without him.'

'Yes, I'm sure, but I imagine it can strain one's finances.'

As if you'd know, thought Saffron, eyeing Heather's perfect ombré French manicure and noting that the bag she'd dropped on the floor beside them was a Burberry.

'Anyway,' said Heather, 'I'd better make tracks. My ten o'clock's a bit tricky and I could do with prep time.'

'Sure,' said Saffron. 'You do you.'

Heather smiled. 'Let me know how it goes.' She leaned down for her bag, then rose and air-kissed Saffron. 'Good luck.'

'Thanks,' said Saffron, automatically.

She sat for some time after Heather had gone.

When the server came to clear the plates, the inch of cappuccino left in her cup was stone cold.

'Was everything all right?' he asked.

Saffron stared at him. She had thought she would be offered a nice package of work at a tempting day rate. Instead, Heather had thrown her a scrap. Working in a general store, for heaven's sake. A minimart. What would that do to her nails?

'With your drinks and—'

'Oh yes,' said Saffron hastily. 'Everything was fine, thanks.' She collected her bag, stood up, and strode out.

She had been offered a job she wouldn't have chosen in a million years. And she had no choice but to take it.

3

'There's nothing to it, really,' said Alf. 'Most of the stuff, you just scan the barcode. If there's no barcode, there should be a price sticker. If there's no price sticker, check the shelf. Once you've rung everything in, you press this button.' He obliged, and the till made a strange sound. A sort of cough, as if it couldn't quite believe what it was hearing. 'You ask if they're paying cash or card. If it's cash, you open the till…'

Saffron felt her mind wandering and snapped to attention.

'Take the cash, entering the amount, and that will tell you how much change to give.'

'And if it's card?'

'Which it is more and more these days. Or sometimes phone, or even smart watch. Like magic, it is. Provided you can get a signal…'

Saffron had considered going home to get changed after her meeting with Heather, since there was no point wasting a Boden top on a minimart. Then she thought *Why should I? They can take me as I am.* So she had merely refreshed her lip gloss in the car park, then jumped up and down a few times, to give herself energy and bounce, and walked in.

'Hello, pet,' said the elderly man behind the counter, who was reading the paper. Presumably, this was Alf. 'Is it windy out?'

'Er, no.' Saffron pushed her hair back.

'So what can I do you for?'

'My friend Heather told me you needed some help.' Saffron stuck out her hand. 'Saffron Montgomery.'

He looked at the hand, then her, and shook it with good grace. 'Hello, Saffron. Heather is the smart lady, isn't she? Always in a rush.'

'That's her,' said Saffron, though actually she thought Heather lacked dynamism.

He chortled. 'I shall feel like a magician with a glamorous assistant!' Before she could moderate that remark, he said, 'Did she tell you what was involved?'

'Yes. Ten till two, five days a week.'

'Can you lift a bag of logs?'

'I beg your pardon?'

'If you can't, it's not too much of a problem. Some customers like us to take it to the car for them, but I daresay we can work something out. A trolley, maybe.'

'Where are the bags?' said Saffron, drawing herself up.

He pointed. 'At the back, left-hand corner.'

Saffron marched through the shop, seized a bag by its scruff, hoisted it onto her shoulder and carried it to the cash register and back. She took her time putting it down, as she was slightly out of breath. 'Happy?' She resolved to practise with the dumbbells at home when the kids were in bed: she seemed to have lost strength since cancelling her gym membership.

Alf whistled. 'Very impressive.'

'Thanks.' Saffron brushed her hands together and strolled to the counter.

'Right, I'll give you the tour, as it's quiet. You've seen the fruit and veg out front. The rest of it is over there.' He gestured to wooden crates filled with cauliflowers, courgettes, and other seasonal produce. 'You'll need to weigh it, and the price per kilo is on here.' He pointed at a list taped to the counter. 'If something's bruised, just give it 'em.'

'Won't people take advantage of that?'

He shrugged. 'Maybe. If they're desperate enough to go to those lengths for a free tomato, I won't deny them.' He came out from behind the counter. 'Baked goods there, ready meals next door, tins in the next aisle, dairy section to the rear and there's a couple of

19

freezers too. Pet supplies in the right-hand corner. Booze at the far end. Newspapers and magazines to the right. Sweets at the counter, with the freezer for ice creams and lollies. Ciggies and vapes behind me, either side of the door to the back of the shop, and here are the lottery tickets and scratch cards.'

'What do you do about ordering stock?' asked Saffron.

'I've got repeat orders set up for the basics. Local farmers and growers usually give us a ring when stuff's coming into season and we take it from there. Don't worry, that's Janet's department.'

'Oh yes,' said Saffron. 'Where is Janet?'

'At chair yoga,' said Alf. 'She's got a gammy leg, but she reckons she can manage that. Then she's helping out at the playgroup. Most days we take it turn and turn about in the shop, with an overlap at lunchtime. Now you're here, hopefully we can spend a bit more time together. Meet friends for lunch, take up some of those hobbies we always said we'd get round to.' He studied Saffron from under shaggy eyebrows. 'So, are you ready for the customers?'

'Oh yes,' said Saffron, with conviction. How hard could it be? She could work the cash register, she knew where everything was, and she'd demonstrated she could lift heavy items. She cracked her knuckles. 'Bring it on.'

'That's the spirit.' Alf reached behind him and

handed her a navy tabard. 'There you go. Ready for action.'

Saffron looked at the tabard as if she was holding a dead fish. 'Surely you don't expect me to wear this.'

'Shops are messy places,' said Alf. 'I wouldn't want you to ruin that nice top.'

Saffron considered, somewhat mollified by Alf's recognition of her top as a quality item. 'I suppose you have a point.' She ran her hand over the nylon, which made a nails-down-the-blackboard screech. 'I'll run the risk,' she said, hanging it on its peg.

Alf shrugged. 'Don't say I didn't warn you.' He looked at his watch. 'I make it five to ten. Cup of tea?'

'Do you have any fruit tea? I only drink caffeine at breakfast.'

'Jan's got camomile tea, would that do?'

'Oh yes, that will be lovely. No milk or sugar.'

Alf's face signalled his opinion of Saffron's beverage preferences. 'I'll see what I can do,' he said, and opened the door to the back.

Saffron lifted the wooden flap which separated the counter from the main shop, took her place behind the counter, and surveyed her new queendom. Vegetables, bread, ready meals, tins, sweets and drinks. *It's four hours a day*, she thought. *Everyone will be busy building empires or changing nappies. I don't even know anyone who lives this far out. If someone does come in, I can say I'm helping as a favour. Surely it can't be that bad.*

She heard Alf whistling and the clink of a teaspoon chasing a teabag round a mug. She hoped that was his teabag he was squeezing to death. *This is just till I get back on my feet. As soon as I do, I'll be gone quicker than you can say business transformation.* And she allowed herself a little smile.

4

Two hours later, Saffron wished she hadn't been so firm about her no-caffeine policy. She had circled the shop numerous times, assembling the contents of Mrs Dawson's shopping list. 'Oh no, not those tomatoes, I like the Napolina ones. Could you get the value baked beans? Those ones you've brought are very expensive. And I may have said wholemeal bread, but I meant spelt.' Saffron had rung everything in, watched Mrs Dawson turn her handbag out on the counter in pursuit of her purse, then count and double-check twenty-pound notes, and had just given her her change when Mrs Dawson remembered that she had forgotten olive oil and cocktail sticks. 'Oh, and once you've done those could you pack the bags and carry them to the car for me? I'm afraid I can't manage them myself.' She held up three hessian shopping bags.

Saffron felt as if her smile would crack her face.

She allowed herself a few choice thoughts as she roamed the store for the missing items, locating the cocktail sticks next to the gin, of all places.

Once the transaction was complete, she left Alf in charge and lugged the bags to the car park, then stood in the hot sun for five minutes waiting for Mrs Dawson to catch up. She sailed over. 'Sorry, my dear, I was having a word with young Alf.' She rummaged in her handbag again and handed Saffron her keys. 'It's the mushroom-coloured one.'

Saffron saw a classic, boxy Mercedes. 'Right,' she said, and loaded the shopping.

'Thank you so much,' said Mrs Dawson. 'Wait a moment.' She took out her purse and handed Saffron a pound coin. 'For your trouble.'

'You don't have to—' But Mrs Dawson was already opening her door. Saffron pocketed the coin and walked into the shop, shaking her head once she was out of view.

Other customers, by comparison, were easy to deal with – in terms of their purchases, at least. However, what should have been quick transactions never were. Everyone had opinions about the weather, the new pothole which had developed not a hundred yards away, the yellow line which had mysteriously appeared outside the community centre, whether Pink Lady or Jazz were the best apples... Often another customer would come in and join the conversation, which lengthened matters still more. At one point, four customers were standing at the counter, goods paid for and change given, still discussing whether the parking spaces by the leisure centre were bound by the same rules as those in the adjoining car park.

Saffron noted that Alf kept the chat going while rarely expressing an opinion himself. When asked, Saffron said what she thought, which was usually met with 'Oh. Well, as I said…' It was more like a game than a discussion: the sort of game where you have to keep all the plates spinning without letting one drop.

Around noon, there was a welcome lull. 'Enjoy it while it lasts,' said Alf. 'It won't be long before the lunch crowd come in. If you need a comfort break, the loo's in back.'

It felt wonderful to close the bathroom door behind her and be on her own for the first time in over two hours. Her hands smelt of coins and plastic. As she washed them, she studied herself in the mirror. The left side of her hair had turned the wrong way and her face was flushed. *Probably all that interaction.* She applied more lipgloss, then found a hair claw and twisted her hair up. At least her top was still clean, though she felt sweaty. *I'll have to buy industrial-strength deodorant. And take a shower as soon as I get home.*

When she came into the shop, Alf said 'Time for lunch.' He walked to the chilled cabinet and took out a ham salad sandwich.

'Oh,' said Saffron. 'I didn't bring anything with me.'

Alf opened the sandwich packet. 'Just grab something off the shelf.'

Saffron's eyes widened. 'Are you sure?'

Alf laughed. 'It's my shop.' He put the packet on the counter, extracted the sandwich and took a hefty bite.

'Thank you.' Saffron went to the cabinet and scanned the contents. Ham salad, cheese salad, egg and cress, BLT... *Salt, fat, carbs...* She inspected the boxed salads and eventually chose an egg salad with a sachet of dressing which she intended to ignore. The shelf label said £1.99. She took the box to the counter, got her bag and rummaged for her purse. 'Two pounds,' she said, putting the coins on the counter.

Alf goggled at her. 'What's that for?'

'Lunch, obviously.'

Alf looked at the money, then at Saffron. 'You don't have to pay for that. If you want to bring your lunch in future, that's fine.'

'Oh. Thanks.' She wasn't sure if Alf was amused or hurt by the situation. She picked up the money and went into the back room for a fork. 'Would you like a drink?' she called.

'Yes please,' Alf replied. 'Strong tea, milk, one sugar.'

Saffron filled the kettle, switched it on and sat down. Working in the shop was harder than she had thought. Not in terms of the work itself – that was hardly taxing – but in navigating what was expected of her. She had assumed that helping herself to the stock would be absolutely forbidden, and here was Alf inviting her to. And she hadn't been prepared for the small talk, the endless small talk… Pretending to be interested in potholes and Mr Jones's begonias and Mrs Watson's collie's stomach—

The kettle clicked off and Saffron realised she hadn't got out mugs, teabags or anything. She hunted in the cupboard above the sink and it was only when she had filled both mugs with hot water that she saw she had given herself a normal teabag. She stared at it in dismay, then shrugged. *It won't kill me. Lord knows I could do with a boost.*

5

Saffron returned with the tea to find Alf chatting with a customer.

'Thanks, pet,' he said, and faced the customer. 'So, are you entering a marrow this year?'

'I'm undecided,' said the customer, a middle-aged man in a checked shirt and jeans. 'I don't have any obvious contenders at the moment. They're all a bit diddy.'

'Can't you feed one up?' asked Saffron. 'Not that I have any idea about growing prize marrows.'

'I could,' said the man. 'But it's a commitment. I might have to sacrifice the others, and there's the danger that it might get nobbled.'

Saffron laughed, then realised he was serious. 'People nobble prize vegetables?'

'It does happen,' said the customer. 'My dad was known for his giant veg, and if he had a really special one, he'd sleep with it for a week before the judging.'

Saffron struggled to keep her face straight. 'I see,' she said, and took refuge in her tea. She sipped, and the hot liquid spread through her veins. She noted wryly that fruit tea didn't have that effect.

'Well, good luck, Jeff, whatever you decide,' said Alf.

'Indeed,' said Jeff. He turned to Saffron. 'Are you a new member of staff?'

'We're trying each other out,' said Alf.

'Yes, we are,' said Saffron, and smiled at Jeff. 'See you again.'

Alf finished his sandwich and went through to the back room with the packaging. When he returned, he asked, 'So, how are you finding it?'

'It's fine,' said Saffron. 'I didn't think people would chat so much.' Then she recalled what Alf had said to Jeff: *We're trying each other out*. Had he introduced her to anyone today? Said she was working here? No, he hadn't. She faced him square on. 'Is there a problem?'

'No, not at all,' said Alf. 'It's just that . . . you don't seem to be enjoying yourself.'

'Oh, I am,' said Saffron. 'I have one of those faces. You know, when you don't look happy even though you are.' She picked up her mug, not exactly to hide behind it.

'Oh, you mean resting bitch face.'

Saffron nearly spat out her tea. 'How do you know about that?'

'Sometimes I flick through one of Jan's magazines,' said Alf, grinning. Then he became serious. 'If the work isn't to your liking, you can say.'

Saffron drank some more tea, to give herself time to think.

Is this what I want to do for four hours every weekday? No.

Do I need the money? Yes.

'This job isn't quite what I thought it would be,' she said. 'But I'm confident I can learn, and if you have any feedback for me, I'd be happy to hear it.'

Alf raised his eyebrows. 'You sure?'

'Of course.' Saffron braced herself.

'In that case...' Alf took a swig of tea. 'Relax, Saffron. You're stiff as a board when you're dealing with the customers, and they can tell. They won't mind if you make a mistake: you're new.'

'Have I made a mistake?'

'No, you've been spot on, and you've remembered all the things I told you. Look, what's your normal line of work?'

Saffron searched for words to explain it in a way that Alf could understand. 'I work with businesses and teams to implement transformational change. Sometimes it's through individual coaching, sometimes with team workshops—'

'A management consultancy sort of thing?'

'Yes,' said Saffron, surprised.

'So you'll understand what I mean when I say that a lot of my customers aren't here for beans and a newspaper. They're here for a chat. Some don't get out much and I'm a friendly face, as is Janet. Some of them make a pitstop between rushing from meeting to meeting, or before dashing home to put their kids to bed. Coming in gives them a chance to switch from business to family mode, so to speak. Even if they just say "Hello, Alf" and we talk about the weather for two minutes. They could stop off at Tesco during the day, or get stuff delivered to their house, but they don't. They come here. In our own way, we're providing a little experience.'

'Understood,' said Saffron. 'So you want me to make conversation with the customers.'

'I just want you to relax, then it will come naturally. You were fine with Jeff, because you were curious about his marrows. It'll be easier when you get to know a few of them.'

'OK,' said Saffron. 'I'll eat my salad before the rush.' She speared a bit of lettuce and half a cherry tomato, put it in her mouth and chewed vigorously. Then she sighed, opened the little sachet of dressing and squeezed it over the rest of the salad. The next mouthful was better. *I am not going to fail*, she told herself. *This is the most basic job I've ever had. I will not be let go.* She forked in mouthful after mouthful, chewing away, until the container was empty. 'Right.' She marched towards the back room with the box.

'For what it's worth,' said Alf, 'you've picked everything up really well. You've been here, what, two hours, and I wouldn't have a problem with nipping out and leaving you in charge.'

'Oh. Good.' She paused. 'Um, what do I do with this? Is there recycling?'

'Yup. Leave it on the side through there and I'll deal with it.'

Saffron did as she had been instructed then washed her hands. As she was drying them, she heard Alf say 'How do, Jamie?'

'Not bad, Alf,' said a vaguely familiar voice.

'How's she coming along?'

'Fits and starts.'

Saffron wondered if they were talking about another giant vegetable. She opened the door to find Mr Sullivan, the caretaker. 'Shouldn't you be at school?' she blurted.

'Lunch break.' He studied her. 'Shouldn't you be organising jumble sales, or fundraising for sports kits?'

'I'm lending a hand in the shop,' she said. 'For a while.'

'That's right,' said Alf. 'This is Saffron's first day with us, and she's doing well.'

'I'm sure *Saffron* is.' He gave her a sly glance. 'A woman with her skills should be an asset to your shop.' She couldn't work out if that was a compliment or an insult.

'I didn't know you knew each other,' said Alf.

'Our paths cross sometimes on the school run,' Saffron said. She eyed his purchases. 'I'm surprised you've come all this way for a BLT and a Coke.'

'It's the excellent service,' said Mr Sullivan. She would *not* think of him as Jamie. He held a card to the machine. The scales of the two fish tattooed on his forearm rippled as the muscles moved. She hadn't noticed before, but the scales were beautifully shaded, ranging from navy to pale orange. He saw her looking, and grinned. 'Admiring my fish?'

'Wondering how long it took to get them,' said Saffron.

'A few visits,' he said. 'I figured the end result was worth it.' He gathered his lunch and the fish rippled again. 'See ya, Alf.'

'Bye, Jamie.' Alf raised a hand as Jamie loped off.

Saffron reached for her mug and found it empty. 'More tea?'

'Don't mind if I do,' said Alf.

The afternoon was busy but uneventful, compared to the morning. Janet turned up, a small slight woman full of apologies, ate a ham salad in the intervals of talking, and left ten minutes later to go to Women's

33

Circle. By quarter to two, Saffron was exhausted from keeping her shoulders down, appearing relaxed, and resisting the urge to initiate conversations and push her opinion. *It's like anti-networking*, she thought. *Hang back, not lean in.*

Alf, who had been pottering round the shelves, returned with a hotchpotch of tins and jars. 'These have got short dates. Can you mark them down to half price? Take a couple, if you want. The pricing gun's under the counter: I'll show you what to do.'

Are you sure? was on the tip of Saffron's tongue. Instead, she said 'Thanks.'

She got to work with the pricing gun, which was surprisingly satisfying, and had the whole collection repriced in a few minutes. She had dismissed most of the tins – the soup would be too salty, tinned ham beyond the pale - but she did pause at the artichoke hearts. Those were definitely out of her reach at their usual price. And she loved artichokes. 'I'll pay you for these.'

'No need,' said Alf. 'Tell me what you cook with them and we'll put a recipe suggestion on the shelf. Don't know why I keep them in, really. I sell a jar once in a blue moon.'

'All right,' said Saffron. 'You're on.'

Alf grinned. 'Bet you didn't think you'd be getting homework. Speaking of which, it's five past two. Off you pop. I'll see you tomorrow.'

'Yes, see you tomorrow.' Saffron got her bag and hurried to the car, clutching her artichoke hearts.

The shower was every bit as welcome as she had anticipated. Saffron rotated beneath the warm water, trying to keep her hair from getting wet. Was she tired? Yes. Had it been as awful as she thought it would be? No. *I'll give it a week. Then I'll know.*

6

And so it began. Every morning, Saffron rose bright and early, did stretching exercises and some light weights, and got ready for the school run before chivvying the children through breakfast, uniforms, and school bags. She had taken to calling them a bit earlier so that they could walk to school, thus avoiding any more confrontations with Mr Sullivan and his tattooed fish.

Once the children were safely in their classrooms, she hurried home and swapped her tight jeans, posh top and heeled boots for wide-leg pants, a T-shirt and trainers. After seeing the state of her nails at the end of the first day, she had trimmed them into short squovals and put on clear varnish. She made sure she had a scrunchie or a hair claw with her, then headed to work.

When she came home, Saffron had a quick shower

and transformed into her usual go-getting deal-making self in time for the school run. This was done in the car, firstly because Aurora and Chad would have after-school activities – swimming, football or a play date – and secondly because after four hours on her feet, she felt she deserved to sit down.

Somehow, she had become the shop's resident chef. She had used the tin of artichoke hearts to make creamy artichoke and spinach pasta, and the children had actually eaten it. Chad had asked what the squidgy things were, but when Saffron replied 'Chopped zombie brains,' that seemed to satisfy him. In fact, he had a second helping.

'Knew you'd manage to do something with them,' said Alf. He rummaged under the counter and produced a large shelf label. 'Write a summary and let's see if we can shift some more.' He tapped the basket of tins on the counter, against which was propped a piece of card saying *HALF PRICE*. 'If you can work out any recipes for what's in there, help yourself and write them up afterwards. I could stop stocking those lines, but I don't like the idea of not having a product that people might want.'

Saffron's brain buzzed with phrases: *Meet the customer where they are*, *Go for the low-hanging fruit* and *Don't spread yourself too thinly*, but she sensed Alf was not about to change his mind. Instead, she browsed the basket and pulled out a dented can of new potatoes. 'I may have an idea for these.' That night she made warm new potato salad and scored another hit.

Once she had recovered from the shock of the first day, work became much easier. She was less focused on not making mistakes, and able to listen to the customers. She remembered a couple of their names and asked after Mrs Watson's collie, who was much better on the Chappie, thank you.

On the third day, Alf disappeared around ten o'clock to work on his allotment. A few minutes later, Janet came in.

'How's the ankle?' Saffron asked.

'Not bad,' said Janet. 'Think my gymnastics days are done.' She grinned. 'You've settled in.'

'Thanks.'

'There isn't much to it,' said Janet. 'It's just keeping the place ticking over. Speaking of which, do you mind if I nip out? I've got a couple of parcels to take to the post office and I'd like to get them in before noon.'

'Yes, of course,' said Saffron. 'That's fine.'

'I'll leave you my mobile number, just in case.'

'I'm sure everything will be—'

But Janet was already scribbling on the small notepad they kept on the counter. 'There you go,' she said, pushing it towards Saffron. 'Put it in your phone, then you won't lose it. What did we do without mobile phones?'

Saffron, who had seen Janet's ancient pink Nokia, merely smiled. 'I know,' she said.

'I shouldn't be too long,' said Janet. 'Unless there's a queue. And I might pop to the library while I'm in town, for that book I requested. Tell you what, if you need me, give me a ring. Alf will probably be back at lunchtime, anyway. Unless he meets one of his gardening pals down the allotment and goes for a pint. Anyway, catch you later.'

As the shop was empty, Saffron allowed herself a big stretch and went to put the kettle on. Automatically, she reached for the PG Tips. The tea made, she strolled around her domain, noting gaps on the shelves, moving stock forward and generally tidying up.

The bell on the door rang and she turned. 'Oh. Hello.'

'Hello,' said Jamie Sullivan. 'Still here, then.'

'I'm holding the fort,' said Saffron. 'Alf and Janet are both out.' She checked her watch. 'Isn't it a bit early for lunch?'

'Day off.' He wandered to the chilled cabinet.

Saffron studied him. He looked just as scruffy as on working days, if not more so. His stubble was darker than usual, his jeans had acquired new black and blue stains and his navy T-shirt was speckled with white. Not that she was examining him with any interest, of course. *Is he painting the whole school? Why doesn't he wear overalls?* Then she glanced at the nylon tabard hanging on its peg and shrugged.

He chose a cheese sandwich and a Diet Coke, which he supplemented with a pack of roast beef Monster Munch. He brought it all to the counter. 'Can I ask you something, Saffron?'

'Ms Montgomery,' she shot back.

He rolled his eyes. 'All right, *Ms* Montgomery. Do your kids know you're working here?'

Heat rushed over Saffron like a forest fire. 'No, they don't!' she snapped. 'This is a temporary job, so they don't need to know. I'm just filling in while – while…'

'There's nothing to be ashamed of.'

'I didn't say there was. But this isn't my usual line of work, and I have no intention of pursuing it for longer than necessary.'

'So it's necessary?'

She studied the counter, unable to meet his eyes. 'For the moment, yes.' She grabbed the sandwich and scanned it, then the drink and crisps. 'Have a nice day.'

'I intend to.' He didn't move. *Why won't he pick up his stuff, get out and leave me in peace?* 'I'm sorry things aren't going well.'

'Things are fine. It's just a temporary lull. Happens in business sometimes.'

'Mmm.' He looked at her. 'Give us a scratch card, would you.'

'Any particular kind?'

'You choose.'

She pursed her lips and considered the options. Nothing stood out, so she chose one at random, garish in yellow and green, and scanned it.

He touched a card to the reader, then picked up his lunch. 'Cheers.'

He was halfway to the door before she realised. 'You forgot your scratch card,' she called.

He looked round. 'That's for you. Maybe your luck will change.' He left, whistling.

Saffron stuffed the scratch card in her handbag, her face burning. *Who does he think he is?* As if a scratch card would change anything. She didn't need luck: she needed an opportunity. The right client would come along – the right *clients* – and everything would go back to normal. *I must work on my manifestation skills. And start putting bids in again.* She stalked to the chiller cabinet and rearranged the sandwiches to fill the gap he had left.

7

Saffron made it through the first week, then the second. She found herself waking before the alarm and wondering who would come in that day. Would Jeff have an update on his marrow, now that he had decided to go for it? How many circuits of the shop would she have to make if Mrs Dawson came in with her list? Which sandwich would Jamie Sullivan choose today?

Sometimes she wandered around the shop, noting unusual foods she could do something with. Alf and Janet always told customers what Saffron had made with various ingredients – tired courgettes which had gone into a parmigiana, tinned ham and leek pie, cauliflower cheese fritters, beetroot hummus – and often customers picked up the item and said they would give it a go. Saffron had begun writing out the recipes so that people could take a picture with their phones. It reminded her of her student days, when she'd made huge pots of stew and veg chilli for her housemates – anything that would fill them up on a budget.

The random assortment of food which Alf and Janet pressed on her had definitely got her out of her cooking rut. Before, it had been a cycle of pasta with sauce and hidden vegetables, veggie burgers and wholemeal buns, mild chicken curry with rice… Perhaps, finally, Aurora and Chad were becoming the adventurous eaters she had always hoped they would be.

She doubted there was any need to exercise in the mornings now, as she got plenty of stretching and weights practice at the shop. But she felt better for it, and the earlier starts meant she could fit in yoga too.

One morning she made French toast for the children, since she had time and an egg to use. Chad wolfed his down. Aurora took a bite then looked at Saffron, a little furrow between her eyebrows.

'What's up?' asked Saffron. 'Don't you like it?'

'I'll eat it if Roar doesn't want it,' said Chad.

'It's lovely, Mummy,' said Aurora. 'Is today a special day?'

'Not particularly,' said Saffron. 'I just thought I'd make a different breakfast.'

'Oh,' said Aurora. She took another bite of the toast. 'Are you shopping at another supermarket?'

'Aurora, you saw the van park outside the other day and you helped me put the food away. You know it's the same supermarket.'

'Something's different,' said Aurora. She took a big bite of her toast, swinging her legs as she chewed.

At the end of the first week, Saffron was surprised when Alf opened the till, counted out some notes and slid them across the counter. 'There you go. Twenty hours at twelve pounds an hour makes two hundred and forty.'

Saffron looked at the money, then picked it up. 'Thank you. I wasn't expecting cash.'

'Well, I *could* ask you for a load of information and fill out all the forms, but I figured you'd rather have the money now. We can sort it out later, if we have to.'

Saffron put the money in her purse, wished him a good weekend and headed to her car. It was only when she was almost home that she realised Alf had paid her more than she expected. Twelve pounds an hour, not eleven. Her throat tightened. *He didn't have to do that*, she thought, and blinked hard.

That weekend, she used some vouchers she had forgotten about and took Aurora and Chad to see the latest Pixar film. She couldn't run to cinema snacks, but she smuggled in bottles of pop and home-made chocolate brownies. She couldn't remember the last time they had gone to the cinema. Probably not since

44

the – since David had moved out of the house and in with *her*. Saffron had been too busy keeping her business going, and lately, she hadn't had the money to spare.

Halfway through the third week, Saffron was alone in the shop, standing on the kick stool and restocking the tinned veg, when the shop bell rang. 'Hello!' she called. 'Do you need any help?'

'I'm looking for vanilla essence,' said a woman's voice.

'It's with the flour in the second aisle,' Saffron called. Then she frowned. *I know that voice.* In her head, she ran through a list of the shop's regulars. It was none of those. The voice was . . . not local. Well spoken, slightly older than her.

'Got it,' said the voice, and heels clicked towards her. 'Can I pay, pl— Oh, it's you!'

Saffron froze. Diana Hargreaves, veteran of a thousand business breakfasts and coaching seminars, was standing in front of her, holding a bottle of vanilla essence and grinning. 'I hardly recognised you in your tabard,' she said.

'What? Oh.' She was only wearing the tabard because Janet had asked if she could come in half an hour early and there wasn't time to change out of the Whistles top she had worn for the school run. There would have been, but she had chatted about a PTA fundraiser with a couple of mums on the playground.

45

Then Jamie Sullivan had caught her as she was leaving to ask whether her 4x4 was petrol or diesel, and how it did for fuel economy. And here she was, with her hair skewered up anyhow and resplendent in a nylon tabard, standing on a kick stool like a monument to shop workers.

She bundled the tins she was holding onto the shelf and climbed down. 'I don't work in this shop, not really. The owner's poorly at the moment, so I said I'd help.'

Diana laughed. 'You certainly look the part. I wondered why I hadn't seen you at Motivation Monday lately.'

I can't afford it. 'I couldn't make it. Booked solid.'

'Oh, that's good,' Diana said easily.

Saffron suspected she didn't believe a word of it. 'Yes, and I must admit that doing this is cramping my style. As soon as the owner's back on her feet, I'll be on the circuit again. I just couldn't leave her in the lurch. Little shops like this are so important for the community, aren't they?'

'Oh yes,' said Diana. 'Now, if I could pay?'

'Of course.' Saffron hurried to the counter. The quicker the transaction was over, the sooner Diana would be gone. 'Cash or card?'

Diana gave her a pitying glance and took out her phone.

Saffron rang up the sale. 'When you're ready.'

Diana touched her phone to the reader. 'What will you be making?'

'I won't.' Diana dropped the little bottle in her bag. 'Minerva is making biscuits in food tech.' She smiled at Saffron. 'Maybe you should keep the tabard: it suits you. See you soon.' She clicked her way to the door.

Seething, Saffron returned to the shelves and shoved the tins into place. What a thing to happen. Hopefully, Diana wouldn't gossip. Hopefully, she was so busy that the encounter would drop out of her head, not to be recalled until Saffron was back on top of her game. Whenever that might be. She hadn't even thought about clients, bids or tenders since starting work at the Country Stores.

Saffron stepped down and nudged the kick stool into the corner with her foot. *Don't get too comfortable*, she told herself, then took off the tabard and hung it on its peg. *This isn't where you belong.* She resolved to get on her laptop and explore opportunities as soon as the kids were settled in bed that evening. Once she'd written up that night's recipe.

8

'So, what are you doing at school today?'

Aurora looked confused. 'Don't you remember, Mummy? It's the school trip!'

'School trip? What school trip?' Saffron had a vision of arriving at school with her daughter to find a coach ready to go and no place for Aurora on it. 'Where to? Was there a letter? Did you bring home a letter? Or was it on the app? I didn't see anything.'

'I brought it home ages ago,' said Aurora. 'We're doing a traffic survey in Meadley. For our topic.'

'Oh. Oh yes.' Saffron closed her eyes and monitored her breathing for a few seconds. 'Do you need anything? A packed lunch? Money?'

'We're having lunch at school as usual, Mummy. Mrs Hanratty said we could bring a pound, so I've got one from my money box.'

'Oh. OK.' Saffron studied her daughter. Usually,

Aurora had no idea what was going on. This was a welcome development. 'So, all sorted, then. Just make sure you're careful around the roads, and do as Mrs Hanratty tells you. What are you doing today, Chad?'

Chad shrugged. 'English. Maths. Something in the afternoon.'

Saffron sighed. At least one of them was up to speed.

She walked the children in and saw them to their respective lines, saying hello to various mums on the way. She wondered where they shopped, what they bought, what they cooked, how much they spent…

'Hello there, *Ms* Montgomery.' It was Jamie, the caretaker. He leaned on the Ms to annoy her, she was sure. 'Nice day for it.'

Saffron looked up. The sky showed a gradient of pale to deeper blue, with a couple of candy-floss clouds to break the monotony. 'Yes, it is.' She smiled. 'A good day for a school trip.'

'Oh, is one of yours off out?'

'Yes, on a traffic survey. I'd better get on.' She glanced about: no one was near. 'The shelves won't stack themselves.'

He grinned. 'Bet you wish they would.' His eyebrows drew together slightly. 'Which one of yours is going on the trip?'

'Aurora, in year five. Mrs Hanratty's class.' He didn't answer. 'I assume you'll be in for your customary sandwich later,' she said, and went on her way.

She glanced back at the gate, and saw him striding towards the school entrance. Her gaze settled on his bottom. *Nice to see you getting a move on for once, Jamie*, she thought, and smirked.

As she drove to the Country Stores, she pondered the mystery of Jamie Sullivan. Why did he come all the way out of Meadley to Alf's shop? He'd have to drive, and there was a petrol station not five minutes' walk from the school which sold perfectly adequate sandwiches. Not that she'd ever eaten one, but they looked OK.

Unless he lives over this way... But in that case, why didn't he call in on his way to work? Or if the shop wasn't open, why not on his way home? That would be a much better use of his time.

She was coming to the double bend in the road, and focused on her driving until she was safely through it. From this point, Meadley opened up into fields and farmland, in the midst of which was The Country Stores. Saffron pulled into the car park, got out and stood for a moment, admiring the view. Beyond the low wooden fence were open fields, with distant, smudgy hills and an occasional spreading tree. In autumn, there would probably be mist. *Lots of people would pay good money for a view like that.* She wondered if Alf and Janet thought much of it.

Then she looked at her watch, a Gucci with a fraying strap, and hurried inside.

Today, Alf was behind the counter. Leaning on it, to be precise. 'Morning,' said Saffron. 'How are you?'

'I've been better,' said Alf, and winced. 'I've pulled my back.'

'Oh no. Have you taken painkillers?'

'I'm waiting to see if it – *ow* – goes off.'

'Oh, *men*.' Saffron opened her bag and found a strip of paracetamol. 'Take two of these, at least.' On the shelves, she found a tube of Deep Heat and a self-heating back wrap. 'Should you be working?' she asked, as she put them on the counter.

'Didn't have a choice. Jan's got an early appointment at the hairdresser and I can't let down the customers.'

'Well, I'm here now…' She paused. 'Speaking of customers, why does Jamie Sullivan come in every day for his lunch? There's loads of other shops nearer the school.'

Alf eased two paracetamol from the blister pack and gulped them with the rest of his tea. 'Maybe it's the excellent service. Maybe he fancies a change of scene. Maybe it's something else.' He twinkled at her. 'And maybe you should ask him, not me.'

'Thanks for nothing,' said Saffron. 'Want another tea?'

'Please. And if you wouldn't mind bringing a chair

with you…'

Saffron fetched a chair and Alf lowered himself carefully into it, landing with an *oof* and another wince. 'How did you pull your back?'

Alf looked shifty. 'I was fetching a sack of sawdust. I twisted to get it through the door, and bingo.'

'I did say you should use a trolley.'

'I suppose,' Alf said, resentfully. 'In my head, I'm still in my twenties. I could have carried three of those then and thought nothing of it.'

'Did you work here in your twenties?'

'I did. My parents owned this place and I was more than happy to take it on. Shame the kids weren't keen.' He shifted slightly in the chair. 'Now, that tea…'

'On it, boss,' she said, and went through to the back.

When she returned with two strong cups of PG Tips, Alf had a list of jobs for her. 'Normally this is done before you turn up,' he said. 'But I decided to do the sawdust first and everything went pear shaped.'

'Just tell me what needs doing, and I'll get to it between customers.'

'First job is to sort out the sack of sawdust stuck in the doorway to the storeroom. Don't even think about lifting it, or you might be on the sick list too. It needs putting in smaller bags. I'll let you work out how best to do it, but I'm telling you now, put the tabard on. That stuff gets everywhere.'

Dealing with the sawdust took a good forty minutes, since it was punctuated by having to dash to the counter and serve people, who all wanted to know why Alf was sitting down and offered various remedies as well as the usual updates and enquiries about today's recipe (fish-finger curry à la Nigella Lawson). Saffron felt as if she was trapped in some sort of Groundhog Day situation as yet another customer said 'What's with the chair, Alf?'

After that, she got on with filling gaps in the shelves, checking for fallen labels, and tidying the chilled cabinet. She was organising the sandwiches when the shop bell rang.

She looked round. 'Typical,' she said, grinning. 'Just as I get this cabinet in order, you come in to mess it up.'

'Nice to see you too,' said Jamie. 'Anyway—'

'You're bright and early. Another day off? No, it can't be – I saw you in the playground.'

'I'm here to tell you something. I'd have come earlier, but a piece of play equipment needed fixing.'

'You've come to tell me something?' She smiled, intrigued.

'The school trip your daughter's on—'

The bell rang as Mrs Hanratty entered the shop. Saffron's jaw dropped. 'Good morning, Alf. Why are you sitting down? Having a rest before the onslaught?' Then she turned. 'Come along, children, we can't stay too long or we'll be late for lunch. Remember, no one is to spend more than a pound. Make your choice quickly, then bring it to the counter and Mr Smith will serve you.'

Children began to file in, tentatively at first. Saffron recognised several of them. *This can't be happening.* She hurried to the rear of the shop and peeped round the shelf. The children had spotted the sweets and converged there, chattering and shrieking. And there was Aurora, coming in with her friend Chloe, with Mrs Luckhurst the teaching assistant bringing up the rear.

She heard footsteps and shrank back. 'Mrs H does this trip every year,' Jamie murmured, 'and she always finishes here.'

Saffron closed her eyes. She felt as if the ceiling might fall on her.

'Stay there,' said Jamie, and strode to the counter. 'Need a hand, Alf? No, don't get up. Just tell me what to do.'

Several of the children said 'Hello, Mr Sullivan,' and Saffron slowly let out a breath.

'Where's Saffron?' said Alf. 'She ought to be serving. Saffron!'

Saffron straightened, uncertain what to do, and glanced at Jamie for guidance. But a voice said

'That's my mummy's name!' and Aurora half ran down the aisle. 'Mummy!' she cried. 'What are you doing here? And why are you wearing a – a shop uniform?'

Jamie reached Saffron first. 'I did try,' he said, putting a hand on her arm.

'I know.' Her breath was coming in gasps. She could hear children whispering, 'That's Roar's mum.'

'Guess you'll have to fess up,' he said, softly.

'Why are you talking to Mr Sullivan? You don't *like* him.' Aurora's voice rang out, clear as a bell. 'And why are you wearing that thing? You don't work here…' Aurora gazed around the shop, at the tins and packets and vegetables and Saffron's handwritten shelf labels, and it was as if a lightbulb switched on above her head. 'Mummy!'

'I—' Saffron swallowed. She looked past Aurora to the counter. Alf was staring at her with a face full of disappointment.

'Go to Mrs Hanratty, Aurora,' she said. 'Choose some sweets.'

'But why—'

'Just go!'

'Thanks a bunch,' said Jamie, and strode towards the counter.

Saffron ripped at the straps of the tabard with a great tearing of Velcro, flung it on the floor, and ran out of the shop. As she rushed to the car, images flicked through her head like playing cards dealt in a pile over and over: Aurora's horror, Alf's disappointment, Jamie's contempt. Horror, disappointment, contempt. And she couldn't fix any of it. She was all out of solutions.

9

Saffron had just reached the car when she realised the major flaw in her escape plan. Her keys, phone and purse were in her bag, which was behind the shop counter.

I can't go back. Not after – that.

But you can't stay here.

I can't face Aurora. Never mind the rest of them.

She recalled that Mrs Hanratty had told the children they couldn't stay long, and Jamie would have to return to school at some point. If she waited until they had gone…

There was literally nowhere to go. The shop was surrounded by fields, and the few buildings within walking distance were at the end of long drives. She imagined herself hiding in a barn, possibly amongst bales of hay. Then she looked at the 4x4 and the low fence beyond. She scrambled over the fence, sank down and put her head in her hands.

What was I thinking? I've been such a fool.

No doubt the children would talk about her on their walk. *It'll be all over the school by home time, and every parent on the PTA will know.* She sniffed, and blinked hard.

If I hadn't made a secret of the shop, I could have put my own spin on it. I could have said I was taking a break. Pivoting. Now everyone will know I work there because I can't make ends meet in my own business.

Which is the truth. Maybe I'm just not good enough at what I do to earn a living in these difficult times. Maybe I was kidding myself all those years, holding forth about clients and journeys and delighting the customer. She certainly hadn't done that today.

She heard high voices chattering in the distance, then the raised voice of Mrs Hanratty, telling the children to stay in pairs and not cross the road till they were told it was safe. Gradually, the voices died away.

What must Aurora think?

I even lied to my children. Well, perhaps I didn't tell them the whole truth—

You lied to them. You told them you were meeting clients when you were working in the shop. That's nothing to be ashamed of: it's honest work that needs doing. They trust you, and look what you did.

I'm a terrible parent…

She curled in a ball and cried, quietly. *If I could change the last quarter of an hour…*

But it goes back further than that. To my attitude, my snobbishness, my belief that I was too good to work in a shop. And it turns out the shop is too good for me.

'Your tractor's still here, so I assume you are too.'

It was Jamie's voice, but there was no warmth in it. 'The children have left and I'm about to, so the coast is clear for you to fetch your bag. I suggest you apologise to Alf while you're there.'

No more banter in the shop, she thought, *and no more chats on the playground.*

She heard the click of a car unlocking, the slam of the door, the growl of an engine.

A minute later, he was gone.

Saffron sat for a while, numb. Then she sighed and got to her feet. Despite the weather, she was shaky, stiff and chilly. Every step towards the shop felt like a step towards her execution.

When she entered, the shop bell rang as if she was just another customer. Alf, still sitting down, glanced her way.

'I'm sorry,' she said. 'I didn't mean—'

Alf held up a hand. 'It's not fair to run out of the shop and leave me with a load of kids. Not with this back.'

59

'I promise I'll nev—'

'Before you start making promises I'm not sure you'll keep, I've texted Jan and she's coming as soon as her hair's set, or whatever they do to it. So you don't need to stay.'

'I want to.'

'You didn't a few minutes ago.'

'I really am sorry.'

Alf didn't reply, or even look at her, and after a few moments she slunk out.

It took two goes to get her key in the ignition. She hoped the roads were quiet: she was in no fit state to drive. *I want to go home.* But home meant going through the village, and it was getting towards lunchtime. Cars would be crawling through, searching for somewhere to park, while people ambled across the road… She shivered at the thought that someone who knew what had happened would see her.

Saffron drove away from the village and parked in a little lay-by beside the river. *What a mess I've made of everything. It's as if the world's against me.*

No: it's you. You're your own worst enemy. None of this would have happened if it wasn't for your stupid pride. Over what? Your disappearing clients and your nonexistent business? Your fancy clothes, until they wear out? This gas-guzzling monster?

She glared at the huge dashboard and remembered Jamie asking about her car's fuel consumption. *If I hadn't messed up, maybe I could have sold it to him.* She pinched the bridge of her nose. *I could still trade it in and get a runabout.*

She closed her eyes and sighed. *Why didn't I think of all this before? And the house eats money.* She tried to tell herself that it was their family home, that she had to keep it for the children's sake, but in truth it felt more like a show home. It was a big house on a good road in a sought-after location: a polished, empty shell. *I'll talk to David about selling it and finding something smaller*, she thought. *But not today.*

She sighed and started the engine.

***

When Saffron drove back to the Country Stores, the car park was empty. She marched to the shop to get it over with. Hopefully it would be like ripping off a plaster: painful, but brief.

Janet was standing behind the counter, looking through a list, with Alf sitting next to her. No customers were near. 'I've come to apologise,' Saffron said. 'Properly. I've been a complete fool and I should have known better. I let pride get the better of me.'

'Alf told me what happened earlier,' said Janet. Her tone was neutral but her expression was set to stern. 'We can't employ an assistant who runs out of the shop, whatever the reason is.'

'I promise I'll never do it again,' said Saffron, 'no matter what happens.'

'You say that now,' said Alf. 'How do we know we can trust you?'

'All I can do is promise. And show you, through hard work.'

Alf considered this. 'You're a good worker, Saffron. I didn't think you would be when you first came. I thought you were too posh to get your hands dirty. I wasn't sure you'd last the week, but you proved me wrong. I assumed you were doing this for a bit of extra cash. Playing at shops.'

'I was at first,' said Saffron. 'I thought it would be easy, and that the work was beneath me. But it isn't,' she added, as Janet bristled. 'To begin with, I saw this job as a way to make easy money till my proper business was back on its feet.'

Janet raised her eyebrows. 'Your proper business?'

'Business consultancy.' Janet's nose wrinkled. 'But working here has made me think differently. I'd like to stay. If you'll have me.'

Alf harrumphed. 'You've apologised, we know you can do the job, and I don't want to have to look for a new assistant—'

'Thank you!' Saffron dived behind the counter and hugged him.

'Steady on!' he said, laughing. 'It's up to Jan as well, not just me.'

'I haven't seen as much of you as Alf has,' said Janet. 'But if he says you're a good worker, I'm prepared to give you another chance.'

'You won't regret it,' said Saffron. 'I promise.' She paused. 'What would you like me to do?' She scanned the shop for gaps to fill, shelves to tidy, surfaces to wipe…

'Go home,' said Alf. 'There's less than an hour of your shift left, and if you haven't already, you should think about what you'll say to your kid. And her teacher.' He raised his eyebrows. 'Not to mention young Jamie. He stayed to help while the kids were here, and while he managed to smile at them, I could tell he was fuming.'

Aurora got it wrong, she wanted to say. But really, she hadn't. She'd seen her mother's offhand, snippy manner with Jamie whenever they met – until recently, at least. What was Aurora meant to think? She only hoped the children hadn't picked up her snobbery too. 'Of course I'll apologise to Jamie. Maybe I can catch him before school finishes.'

'Probably best to let him get on with things for a bit,' said Alf. 'He's got a lot on his plate at the moment. Maybe a quick apology if you happen to see him, then leave it for a day or two. Or when he comes in next. Oh, and, er…'

'Yes?' Saffron stood poised.

'You might want to go in the back and wash your face.' Alf looked bashful. 'I hate to say it, but you're a bit, um…'

Janet nodded vigorously. 'I didn't like to mention, but you look a right state.'

Saffron grimaced at her reflection in the bathroom mirror. Her supposedly waterproof mascara was streaked down her cheeks and her nose and eyes were red from crying. Gently, she washed away the black trails and regarded herself in the mirror. Normally, she would grab her make-up bag and repair the damage by slapping on another layer, but now it didn't matter. Her priority was to do whatever it would take to put things right.

10

Saffron walked along the road to school, dreading what was to come.

When she had finally checked her phone, an hour before pickup time, she found a voicemail from school. 'Hello, this is Mrs Hanratty, Roar's teacher. Please could you come to pickup fifteen minutes early. I'd like a word.'

A pause. Saffron hoped she was about to say 'You're not in trouble.'

'Please can you let the office know whether you can make it. Thank you.'

Saffron deleted the message, then rang school to say that she would be there. 'Thank you,' sing-songed whoever was on reception. *Glad you're so pleased*, thought Saffron. *At least it isn't the headteacher. Yet.*

She reached the gate, let herself in and walked round to the junior playground. Thankfully, Jamie wasn't on patrol. *I can't face him, not yet. And I have to talk to Aurora and Chad first.*

The classroom windows were covered with tinted film, but she could just see heads bent over pieces of paper. She was about to tap on the window when Mrs Hanratty opened the door. 'Ten minutes left, class,' she said. 'Ask Mrs Luckhurst if you need more paper.' She let the door fall to, then walked to a bench a short distance away. Saffron followed.

'I'm so sorry about this morning,' said Saffron. 'If I'd known you were coming…'

'I wish you'd said something beforehand,' said Mrs Hanratty. 'Either to Roar, or to me.'

'I suppose they've been talking about it all day.' Saffron looked at her feet.

'What they have been talking about is you doing a runner. None of them understand, because they think working in a shop where there are sweets and crisps and fizzy drinks is a cool job. Whatever you may think of it.'

'It's – it's a nice job. I enjoy it. But it's not what I saw myself doing.'

'When I was a kid, I wanted to be lead singer in a band.' Mrs Hanratty leaned back on the bench. 'I practised in front of the mirror until I drove my family round the bend. I did GCSE music, then A-level, and auditioned for loads of local groups. Unfortunately, they didn't want a short, plump lead singer. I tried forming my own, but I couldn't get that off the ground either. And no, that wasn't fair. So instead, I run a choir and I'm the school's subject lead for music. It's not my dream, but I still get to do what I love and help other people enjoy it too.'

'I'm sorry,' said Saffron.

'I'm not,' said Mrs Hanratty. 'Not now. I can't imagine myself on a tour bus, and my kids would miss me.' For a moment, she looked a bit misty-eyed. 'Anyway, I told Roar earlier that you'd phoned and you were OK.'

'Is she OK?' *That should have been the first thing I asked.* She wanted to smack her own forehead.

Mrs Hanratty smiled. 'She was worried about you. I don't think she minds you working in a shop at all. She was just puzzled as to why you hadn't told her. You will explain to her, I take it?'

'Yes, of course.'

'Good. She's said sorry to Mr Sullivan. Not that that was really her fault.'

'I'll be apologising to him too,' said Saffron. She sighed. 'I have a lot of climbing down to do.'

'Don't be too hard on yourself,' said Mrs Hanratty. 'People will understand.' She stood up. 'I'd better go and put them out of their misery. Nothing like a surprise test to take their mind off things.'

People were drifting into the playground. Some waved to Saffron, and she waved back. *Would they be waving if they knew?* Then she shrugged. *If they don't want to talk to me because I work in a shop, it's their loss.*

The bell rang. Saffron faced the classroom door.

***

'So does that mean we get free stuff?' asked Chad, for the third time.

'Not all the time,' said Saffron. 'It's a perk of the job. And no, that doesn't include sweets.' She sighed. 'I should have told you at the start. That would have been the sensible thing to do, but even grown-ups aren't always sensible.'

'We know that, Mummy,' said Aurora. 'Our teachers are silly sometimes. Like when they wear costumes for World Book Day or play pranks on each other.'

'Yes, but that's fun silly,' said Saffron. 'Not silly silly, which is what I was. I didn't lie, exactly, but I didn't tell you the whole truth. I was embarrassed that we needed the money. But the price of everything is rising, so I had to do something, and this came along, and—'

'It's all right, Mummy,' said Aurora. She got down from the breakfast bar, came round to Saffron and reached up for a hug.

'If anyone's ever mean to you because of it, tell me. Or your teacher.' Mrs Hanratty would sort the kids out far more effectively than she could, she thought wryly. So much for those communication seminars.

'They won't be. Everyone wants to know whether you get to push the buttons on the big cash register and put prices on things with one of those sticker guns.'

Saffron laughed. 'Yes. Yes, I do. Maybe, if it fits in with what you're learning, you could visit the shop again and we could show you.'

'Wow,' breathed Aurora.

'Mum…' said Chad.

'Yes?' Saffron said warily. *I've been so busy making sure Aurora's all right. Have I neglected Chad? He's not traumatised, is he?*

'What's for tea?'

She wasn't sure whether she wanted to laugh or cry most. 'I don't know. To be honest, I haven't thought.' She looked in the fridge, then the cupboard. 'How about . . . risotto?'

'With cheese on top?'

'Yes, with cheese on top.'

He grinned and gave her a thumbs up.

***

Saffron woke early the next morning. As she was doing her morning yoga, she pondered the contents of her wardrobe. *Boden? Whistles? White Stuff?*

What's the point? You may as well save those for going out.

Yes, but... I'll feel better if I can hide behind my glam mum uniform.

Which you've been doing far too long. You're still you, whatever you wear.

So Saffron put on one of her shop tops and her black wide-leg trousers. She put her hair up, and restricted herself to tinted moisturiser and one coat of mascara. *He's seen me in shop clothes loads of times,* she thought, as she filled the toaster. *He won't care what I'm wearing.* She blinked, pressed her lips together and got the butter and jam from the fridge.

She walked the children to school with her head held high, ready to be ignored, ostracised and whispered about. However, as far as she could tell, everyone was busy getting their children to school on time and with all their belongings. *You idiot. Thinking you'd be the centre of attention.*

In the playground, the same people as usual said hello. Then she felt a tap on her shoulder and turned.

'Hello there,' said Heather, with a wry smile. 'I believe word's got out.'

'It has,' said Saffron. 'Which is OK.'

'Good.' Heather looked relieved.

'Thank you for recommending me in the first place. I'm not sure I thanked you at the time, but I've learnt a lot.'

'About running a shop?'

'And other things too.'

70

Someone vaguely familiar was heading over. As she moved closer, Saffron recognised Becca.

'Hi,' Becca said, shifting from foot to foot, and Saffron wondered what was coming next. 'Ellie says one of her classmates told her her sister said you were working at the Country Stores.'

The grapevine's in full working order. 'Yes, that's right,' said Saffron, trying not to sound abrupt.

'I came to say that . . . if you ever want to talk shops, we could maybe swap ideas?' She was so timid and hesitant that Saffron could have hugged her.

'That would be great,' she said. 'There's a lot you can teach me.'

Becca's eyes widened and she beamed. 'I'll send you a text.'

The bell rang, and Saffron watched the lines of children file into classrooms as their parents drifted towards their destiny for the day. She sighed. *Time to face Jamie.*

11

Saffron walked slower and slower as she neared the school entrance. The door was locked, so she pressed the door buzzer. 'Yes?' the intercom crackled.

'It's Saffron. Saffron Montgomery.'

'How can I help?' The voice sounded like Angie. Saffron had the distinct impression that Angie wasn't keen on her, though she wasn't sure why. *Probably my fault.*

She brushed that aside for the moment. 'I wondered if I could speak to J— To Mr Sullivan. The caretaker.'

'One moment.' A phone was ringing in the background. The intercom went dead for a couple of minutes, then came back to life. 'Sorry about that,' Angie said perkily. 'What was it you wanted?'

'Can I speak to Mr Sullivan, if he's available.'

'Ah. Sorry, he isn't in today.'

'Not in?'

'No, he has a day off,' Angie said, as if explaining to a child.

'Oh.' Saffron became conscious of a heavy feeling in her chest. *It's Friday. I can't hang on to this all weekend.* 'It's just that – it's important.'

'May I ask what it's concerning?'

A number of replies to Angie's question flashed through Saffron's mind, none appropriate in a school setting. 'It's… It's not a school matter.'

'Ohhhhhh.' While Saffron couldn't see Angie through the glass door, she was pretty sure she was grinning like the Cheshire Cat. 'Actually, he *did* leave a message . . . where is it, now…'

Saffron's heart thumped. What would the message be? She imagined the intercom crackling into life and Angie reading out: *You are the rudest, most ungrateful person I've ever met*, or *Please don't talk to me ever again*, or *I'm taking my business to another shop.*

'Here we are,' said Angie. 'He said, "If anyone comes looking for me today on a non-school matter, I'm at the Icon gallery in Meadborough this morning." There you go, Ms Montgomery. Have a good day.' The intercom went dead.

Saffron checked her watch. If she hurried home and got straight in the car, she could make it to Meadborough and back and not be late for work.

73

Thank heavens I didn't put those stupid boots on, she thought, as she ran.

***

By some kind of miracle, the traffic was light. Saffron was in Meadborough and parked by twenty-five past nine. The Icon Gallery, where she had bought a couple of paintings and now visited just to look, was a short walk away. She got an hour's free ticket and ran.

She had been so focused on getting to the gallery that she hadn't given any thought to why Jamie was there. Did he do painting and decorating on the side? That would explain the state of his clothes. Being a caretaker couldn't pay much, so she didn't blame him.

The door of the gallery was open, but the windows were covered with dust sheets. *Yup, redecorating.* A piece of paper was stuck in the middle of the window. *That'll be to say when they reopen*, she thought, glancing at it.

OPENING TOMORROW
RURAL ROMANCE:
PAINTINGS BY JAMIE SULLIVAN

Her eyes widened. *But—*

The paint-stained jeans. Driving to the middle of nowhere every lunch break. Alf's caginess about what Jamie might be doing.

And you never worked it out, because the school caretaker couldn't possibly be a painter. She thought of what Mrs Hanratty had told her the day before. Then she recalled the end of year concerts, the school orchestra, the school music competition, and her face flamed. *I'll say my piece and go.*

The gallery was cool and seemed empty. The lights were on, though, and a few paintings were already hung. Saffron's feet took her towards them.

There was the Country Stores, its lights on, a little beacon in a rolling landscape of dark fields and hills. A huge farm machine loomed among wildflowers. A woman roamed in a field of corn. She had long brown hair with blonde highlights, and wore a striped top and jeans…

She heard voices, and Dan the gallery owner entered from the back. 'Oh, hello, um…'

'Saffron Montgomery. I've bought from you before.'

'Oh yes, of course. I'm afraid we aren't actually open—'

Jamie appeared in the doorway. 'It's OK, Dan. Would you mind if I took a quick break?' He was wearing his usual scruffy jeans and T-shirt. She couldn't tell what he was thinking.

Dan raised his eyebrows. 'Someone from the local paper's coming at ten to ten.'

'So we've got a few minutes.'

'Sure,' said Dan, and strode off, shoulders tense.

Jamie walked to the furthest corner of the shop and Saffron followed. 'I assume you've come out here for a reason,' he said, his face still neutral.

'I'm so sorry about what happened yesterday,' she said. 'I don't hate you or dislike you, not at all. I used to, and it was stupid of me, but now I know better. Thank you for helping, even though it was my own fault.'

'Uh-huh.' He stood, looking at her. 'Apology accepted,' he said, and smiled.

'It wasn't Aurora's fault,' she said. 'It was mine. Please don't be hard on her.'

'Wouldn't dream of it. Kids make mistakes all the time.'

'Not just kids. I really am sorry. If there's anything I can do…'

'Half price on everything in the shop?' He grinned.

Saffron returned the grin. 'That's for Alf and Janet to decide.' She glanced about her. 'I hadn't realised you were a painter. An artist, I mean.'

'It's not something that comes up when I'm telling you off for parking where you shouldn't,' he said. 'When I took the caretaker job a few years back, I decided to keep the art stuff out of it. I didn't want to be one of those people who talk up their side hustle and neglect their job. Although it does sneak in.'

76

'How?'

'Well, I run an art club, and sometimes Mrs Patterson, the subject lead, asks me to help with the older kids. She's part-time, so it means the kids don't miss out. I was working with your lad the other day. Chad, is it? He's pretty good.'

Saffron recalled her attempts at school conversation with Chad. *Dunno. Something after lunch.* 'Which I'd know if he ever talked about school.'

Jamie grinned. 'Not just your kids.'

A cough came from the other side of the gallery. 'I think Dan's trying to drop a hint,' said Jamie. 'And you've got a shop to run.'

Saffron glanced at her watch. 'Oh heck, yes I have.'

Jamie took a flyer from a nearby table and gave it to her. 'If you fancy it, we open tomorrow. Bring the kids, if you want. Tell them I said hi.'

'I will.' She waited for him to say goodbye, to move off, but he didn't. 'That picture, of the woman in the cornfield... She looks like me.'

He bit his lip. 'She does a bit, doesn't she?'

She smiled. 'Since you're an art megastar, I assume you'll be wined and dined for lunch today?'

He laughed. 'Nah. I'll be here this morning, then coming to the shop for my usual.'

'In that case, I'll save you a BLT. I really must go. Catch you later.' She made to pat his shoulder in farewell, but he moved and she touched his arm, warm and muscular. A tingle spread right through her.

She hurried to the car, feeling as if she must be glowing like a lightbulb. She was still holding the flyer. She tried to shove it in her bag, but something was in the way. *What's in there?* She put her hand in and her fingers brushed cardboard. She pulled out the scratch card Jamie had given her and stared at it, then grinned. *Why not?*

She got in the car, found a coin in the cupholder and rubbed. *No . . . no . . . no— Wait...*

Saffron stared at the little piece of card, unable to believe what she was seeing. She took a couple of deep breaths, pulled her phone from her bag and dialled.

12

'Roar! Chad! Time for breakfast!' Saffron paused, for effect. 'Otherwise I'll have to eat all these pancakes myself.'

A few seconds later, two doors slammed upstairs and the children came clattering down. 'Cheers, Mum,' said Chad, as he jogged past.

'Don't mention it.' She'd known that pancakes would get them out of bed. She definitely didn't want them being late on the first day of the new school year.

'I can't believe I'm in year six,' said Roar. 'Top of the school.'

'Yes, and you'll have to set an example,' said Saffron. 'Being as you're deputy head girl.'

Roar grimaced. 'Don't remind me.'

'You'll be fine.' Saffron reached over and ruffled her hair. 'Now eat up.' She took a pancake for herself and added sugar, lemon and banana slices.

'Are you at the shop today, Mum?' asked Chad.

'I am in the morning. In the afternoon, Alf and I are speaking to a group of local business owners about community outreach and reducing food waste.'

'Wow,' said Roar. 'That's cool.'

Saffron smiled. 'I suppose it is.'

Once everyone was ready, Saffron led the way past Taylor, the small red electric car on the drive, and they set off for school. The children surged ahead, calling to friends and running to catch them.

Saffron strolled, enjoying the slight chill in the air, welcome after a baking summer. Doing the school run seemed a bit pointless now that the children were perfectly capable of going on their own, but she wasn't ready to give it up yet. And of course, there was Jamie.

Today he was mending the fence, wrapping tape round some broken wires.

'Morning,' she called.

He gave her a cheeky grin. 'Good morning yourself.' He held her gaze until the mass of parents and children squeezing by threatened to send her flying.

'I'd better go,' she said, giggling, and allowed the stream to carry her along. *He'll be in later, anyway.*

She went to the junior playground and checked the children were where they should be and still in possession of their school bags, then kissed them both and stood back. Chad slouched as usual, but Roar stood tall. *Don't worry too much about the responsibility, Roar*, thought Saffron. *Don't forget to have fun.*

As she left, she waved to a few people she knew, including Becca. They had met for a quick chat at the end of the summer term, half an hour before school pickup, and done some video chats over the holidays. *One day I'll be able to go out in the evenings and see friends.* Then she thought of the weekend to come and smiled. *Got to earn the pennies first.* She walked home, got into Taylor, and drove the nippy little car to the Country Stores.

'Howdy, partner,' said Alf, who was sitting at the counter pricing tins.

'Howdy,' said Saffron, with a grin.

***

The first thing she had done after playing the scratch card was to phone the shop. 'Something odd's happened, Alf,' she said. 'It's good, but I'll be a bit late. I'll tell you when I get in.'

Saffron walked to the gallery. Through the glass panel in the door she could see Tim, the nice reporter from the *Meadborough and District Times*, talking to Dan. Jamie stood near, arms folded. She opened the door and went in.

Jamie gave her a quizzical look. 'Shouldn't you be

at work?' he whispered.

Saffron handed him the scratch card. He glanced at it, his eyebrows shot up, and he whistled.

Dan and Tim glanced round. *Sorry*, he mouthed.

He took Saffron to the other end of the room and handed back the scratch card. 'You've got that luck you needed, then,' he murmured.

'I can't take it,' Saffron whispered. 'It's yours.'

'I gave it to you.'

'What are we going to do? Are you really telling me that you don't want the money?'

He shrugged. 'It isn't mine.'

'How about we split it?'

Jamie considered this. 'OK,' he said, eventually. 'If you change your mind, that's all right. You've got kids to worry about.'

'Half each,' said Saffron, and stuck out her hand.

'You're on,' Jamie said, and shook it.

It wasn't life-changing money, not for either of them. But it was enough to make things considerably more secure. Saffron put some away for the children, some into savings, and treated herself to a couple of luxuries. With the rest, she bought a share in the Country Stores. And she carried on working there.

***

As usual, the morning flew. Now that Jeff's marrow had won first prize at the county show, he was considering what giant autumnal veg he could grow. Several people had harvested more apples than they knew what to do with, and wanted Saffron's help to use them before they went bad. On top of that, the trolley for moving heavy goods had a loose wheel which needed attention.

Saffron was wiping her hands on a cloth when Jamie walked in. 'Got any sarnies left?'

'We're down to egg and cress.' She laughed at his disappointed face. 'There's a tomato, mozzarella and basil one hiding in the corner.'

'Lovely.' He walked over and claimed it, with a packet of ready-salted crisps and a bottle of 7-Up. 'Still on for Saturday?'

'Oh yes.' Saffron went to the counter and rang up the purchases.

The children had been annoyed that they would miss out on a day trip. 'Why does Dad have to have us this weekend?' grumbled Chad.

'Don't be silly,' said Saffron, 'you'll have a great time. Aren't you going to that Minions movie?'

'Oh yeah,' said Chad. 'S'pose.'

Jamie was taking her to Meadingley Magna, a little village about twenty miles away. Weather permitting, they would stroll, scout for new painting subjects, and have a picnic. There might even be scope for a lunchtime drink at the village pub.

'Would you mind if I took sketching gear?' asked Jamie. 'Not to draw for hours, just to get some

83

impressions.'

'Fine by me,' said Saffron. 'I'll bring a book.'

The corners of his mouth curled up in a way she found hard to resist. 'Would you mind if I sketched you?'

'I'll have to think about that.'

Saffron imagined herself in a gallery, or on someone's wall. It would be Jamie's achievement, not hers, but she didn't mind at all.

What To Read Next

Tales of Meadley is a sidestep for me, as I usually write mysteries! However, I have suggestions…

If you love modern cozy mysteries set in rural England, *Pippa Parker Mysteries* is a six-book series set in and around the village of Much Gadding.

In the first book, *Murder at the Playgroup*, Pippa is a reluctant newcomer to the village. When she meets the locals, she's absolutely sure. There's just one problem: she's eight months pregnant.

The village is turned upside down when a pillar of the community is found dead at Gadding Goslings playgroup. No one could have murdered her except the people who were there. Everyone's a suspect, including Pippa…

With a baby due any minute, and hampered by her toddler son, can Pippa unmask the murderer?

Find *Murder at the Playgroup* here: http://mybook.to/playgroup.

If you like modern cozy mystery with older characters and a spot of romance, you might like the *Booker & Fitch Mysteries* series I write with Paula Harmon.

As soon as they meet, it's murder!

When Jade Fitch opens a new-age shop in the picturesque market town of Hazeby-on-Wyvern, she's hoping for a fresh start. Meanwhile, Fi Booker is trying to make a living from her floating bookshop as well as deal with her teenage son.

It's just coincidence that they're the only two people on the boat when local antiques dealer Freddy Stott drops dead. Or is it?

The first book in the series is *Murder for Beginners*: https://mybook.to/Beginners.

Acknowledgements

As always, my first thanks go to my super beta readers – Carol Bissett, Ruth Cunliffe, Paula Harmon and Stephen Lenhardt. Thank you so much for your help! Any errors that remain are of course my responsibility.

If you're suspicious of Saffron's recipe creations, they can all be found on the web – and I heartily recommend Nigella Lawson's fish-finger bhorta! You can find the recipe here: https://www.nigella.com/recipes/fish-finger-bhorta (we tend to put a bit more veg in to bulk it out). An extra thank you goes to Paula for coming up with a tinned ham recipe…

And many thanks to you, dear reader! I hope you've enjoyed the latest tale of Meadley. If you have, please consider leaving a short review or a rating on Amazon and/or Goodreads. Reviews and ratings are very important to authors, as they help books to find new readers.

COVER CREDITS

Font: Allura by TypeSETit. License: SIL Open Font License v1.10: http://scripts.sil.org/OFL.

Cover illustration by me (see copyright page).

About Liz Hedgecock

Liz Hedgecock grew up in London, England, did an English degree, and then took forever to start writing. After several years working in the National Health Service, some short stories crept into the world. A few even won prizes. Then the stories started to grow longer…

Now Liz travels between the nineteenth and twenty-first centuries, murdering people. To be fair, she does usually clean up after herself.

Liz's reimaginings of Sherlock Holmes, the Magical Bookshop series, the Pippa Parker cozy mystery series, the Caster & Fleet Victorian mystery series and the Booker & Fitch mysteries (written with Paula Harmon) and the Maisie Frobisher Mysteries are available in ebook and paperback.

Liz lives in Cheshire with her husband and two sons, and when she's not writing or child-wrangling you can usually find her reading, messing about on Twitter, or cooing over stuff in museums and art galleries. That's her story, anyway, and she's sticking to it.

You can also find Liz here:

Website/blog: http://lizhedgecock.wordpress.com
Facebook: http://www.facebook.com/
lizhedgecockwrites
Twitter: http://twitter.com/lizhedgecock
Instagram: https://www.instagram.com/lizhedgecock/
Goodreads: https://www.goodreads.com/lizhedgecock

Books by Liz Hedgecock

To check out any of my books, please visit my
Amazon author page at http://author.to/LizH. If you
follow me there, you'll be notified whenever I release
a new book.

The Magical Bookshop (6 novels)
An eccentric owner, a hostile cat, and a bookshop
with a mind of its own. Can Jemma turn around the
second-worst secondhand bookshop in London? And
can she learn its secrets?

Pippa Parker Mysteries (6 novels)
Meet Pippa Parker: mum, amateur sleuth, and
resident of a quaint English village called Much
Gadding. And then the murders begin…

Booker & Fitch Mysteries (5 novels, with Paula Harmon)
Jade Fitch hopes for a fresh start when she opens a
new-age shop in a picturesque market town.
Meanwhile, Fi Booker runs a floating bookshop as
well as dealing with her teenage son. And as soon as
they meet, it's murder…

Caster & Fleet Mysteries (6 novels, with Paula
Harmon)

There's a new detective duo in Victorian London . . .
and they're women! Meet Katherine and Connie, two
young women who become partners in crime. Solving
it, that is!

Mrs Hudson & Sherlock Holmes (3 novels)

Mrs Hudson is Sherlock Holmes's elderly landlady.
Or is she? Find out her real story here.

Maisie Frobisher Mysteries (4 novels)

When Maisie Frobisher, a bored young Victorian
socialite, goes travelling in search of adventure, she
finds more than she could ever have dreamt of.
Mystery, intrigue and a touch of romance.

The Spirit of the Law (3 novellas)

Meet a detective duo – a century apart! A modern-day
police constable and a hundred-year-old ghost team
up to solve the coldest of cases.

Sherlock & Jack (3 novellas)

Jack has been ducking and diving all her life. But
when she meets the great detective Sherlock Holmes
they form an unlikely partnership. And Jack discovers
that she is more important than she ever realised…

Tales of Meadley (3 novelettes)
A romantic comedy series based in the village of Meadley, with a touch of mystery too.

Halloween Sherlock (3 novelettes)
Short dark tales of Sherlock Holmes and Dr Watson, perfect for a grim winter's night.

For children
A Christmas Carrot (with Zoe Harmon)
Perkins the Halloween Cat (with Lucy Shaw)
Rich Girl, Poor Girl (for 9-12 year olds)

WHITE
RHINO
BOOKS

Printed in Great Britain
by Amazon